Cinnamon Baby

For Audie, my cinnamon baby, and her Grandmother Jean — N.W.

To Élodie and Gilles and their beautiful little girl Zoé — J.N.

Text © 2011 Nicola Winstanley
Illustrations © 2011 Janice Nadeau

All rights reserved. No part of this publication may be reproduced, stored in a retrieval system or transmitted, in any form or by any means, without the prior written permission of Kids Can Press Ltd. or, in case of photocopying or other reprographic copying, a license from The Canadian Copyright Licensing Agency (Access Copyright). For an Access Copyright license, visit www.accesscopyright.ca or call toll free to 1-800-893-5777.

Kids Can Press acknowledges the financial support of the Government of Ontario, through the Ontario Media Development Corporation's Ontario Book Initiative; the Ontario Arts Council; the Canada Council for the Arts; and the Government of Canada, through the BPIDP, for our publishing activity.

Published in Canada by
Kids Can Press Ltd.
25 Dockside Drive
Toronto, ON M5A 0B5

Published in the U.S. by
Kids Can Press Ltd.
2250 Military Road
Tonawanda, NY 14150

www.kidscanpress.com

Kids Can Press is a *Corus*™ Entertainment company

The artwork in this book was rendered in watercolor, graphite pencil and paper collage and assembled digitally.
The text is set in BeLucian Book.

Edited by Tara Walker
Designed by Karen Powers

This book is smyth sewn casebound.

Manufactured in Shen Zhen, Guang Dong, P.R. China, in 10/2010 by Printplus Limited

CM 11 0 9 8 7 6 5 4 3 2 1

Library and Archives Canada Cataloguing in Publication

Winstanley, Nicola
Cinnamon baby / written by Nicola Winstanley ; illustrated by Janice Nadeau.

ISBN 978-1-55337-821-1

I. Nadeau, Janice II. Title.

PS8645.I57278C55 2011   jC813'.6   C2010-904765-6

Cinnamon Baby

Nicola Winstanley

Janice Nadeau

KIDS CAN PRESS

There once lived a baker called Miriam.
Every day except Sunday, she would wake
before sunrise and ride her bicycle
to her own little bakery.

There she would make wonderful bread, full of smells to make your nose twitch and tastes to make your tongue tingle. She made a spicy bread, studded with little peppercorns and basil, and a sweet bread with ginger. She made a light, white loaf with dill, and a crusty brown one with sunflower seeds and honey.

Miriam loved to take the springy dough from
the mixer and knead in all the tasty treasures with her warm,
soft hands. Because it was her favorite, Miriam always saved
the cinnamon bread for last. As she kneaded the raisins into
the dough, she sang all the songs her mother had taught her when
she was a child, and the smell of cinnamon and the sound of
her beautiful voice rose together and
curled through the air.

One cool autumn morning a man called Sebastian was passing
Miriam's bakeshop when her sweet-smelling voice came floating
through the window. He went inside the shop and bought some
cinnamon bread. After that he bought a loaf of bread every
day for a year. Then he asked Miriam if she would
marry him, and she said yes.

Before long Miriam was going to have a baby. As her belly
grew she continued to mix and knead and bake, always saving
the cinnamon bread for last so that the smell lingered until
closing time, when she would take off her apron and
gather her things and go home with Sebastian.

When the baby was born Miriam and Sebastian
were very happy. The child had big brown eyes and
dusky skin and smelled like sweet milk.

For three days Miriam stayed in bed with the baby,
and for three days the baby gurgled and hiccuped and
sneezed and cooed and kicked its tiny legs in the air.
Miriam was sure the baby smiled at her. Sebastian knew
it was the most beautiful and perfect child that had ever
been born.

On the fourth day, the baby started to cry. Miriam held the baby against her breast, but the crying continued. She jiggled it, sang to it, rocked it and walked it up and down and up and down the hallway. But still the baby cried.

The baby was still crying when Sebastian
got home. He held the baby upside down, he
bathed it, he tickled it and he played with
its toes. But nothing did any good.

The baby cried for twelve hours.
Then it finally fell asleep.

But when the baby woke up, it started to cry once more. So Miriam dressed the baby, put it in the baby carriage and went for a walk.

The baby cried at the sky. It cried at the flowers.
It cried at the sunshine and the wind in the trees
and at everyone who passed.

Miriam took the baby to see the doctor.
"The baby is not sick," he told her. "I think it
is simply unhappy." But no one knew why.

Sebastian got home later that day, and the baby was still crying. He wrapped it up in a soft blanket and walked through the chilly streets with the baby crying in his arms. The baby cried at the moon and the stars and the streetlights and the darkness. Finally the baby fell asleep, and Sebastian went home and they both tucked in to bed beside Miriam.

When Miriam woke up, the house was silent. She looked down at her beautiful sleeping child, curled up, knees to chin. The baby reminded Miriam of a little, wrinkled raisin, and she leaned close and breathed in the baby's sweet milky smell.

"Wake up!" she whispered to Sebastian suddenly.
"Wake up! There's something I have to do."

The baby woke up, too, and Miriam gathered up the crying
child and they all went out into the still-dark morning.

By the time they arrived at the bakery, the sun had begun to rise. Everything glowed pink and there was no sound except the endless wail of the unhappy child.

Miriam immediately set to work, measuring and pouring flour and yeast and sugar and milk. The mixers began to beat the ingredients with a loud whoosh. Under its familiar sound, the baby's crying seemed a little softer.

Once the dough had started to rise, Miriam took it out of the mixing bowl and began to knead it. Thumping and pushing the dough to the rhythmless sound of the baby's crying, Miriam made every kind of bread she could think of, with every herb and spice on the bakery shelf: basil, coriander, ginger and allspice, parsley, oregano, rosemary and sea salt, chili, paprika, sage and nutmeg.

Finally, because she always saved it for
last, Miriam made the cinnamon bread.
And what do you think happened?

As soon as the little bakery began to fill with the cinnamony smell of the dough, the baby stopped crying ... and smiled. Then it slipped into a blissful sleep as its mother sang, and her voice and the smell and the warmth from the oven and the taste of sugar in the air filled all the child's senses.

And each day afterward, Miriam made cinnamon bread and the baby was happy and never cried like that ever again.

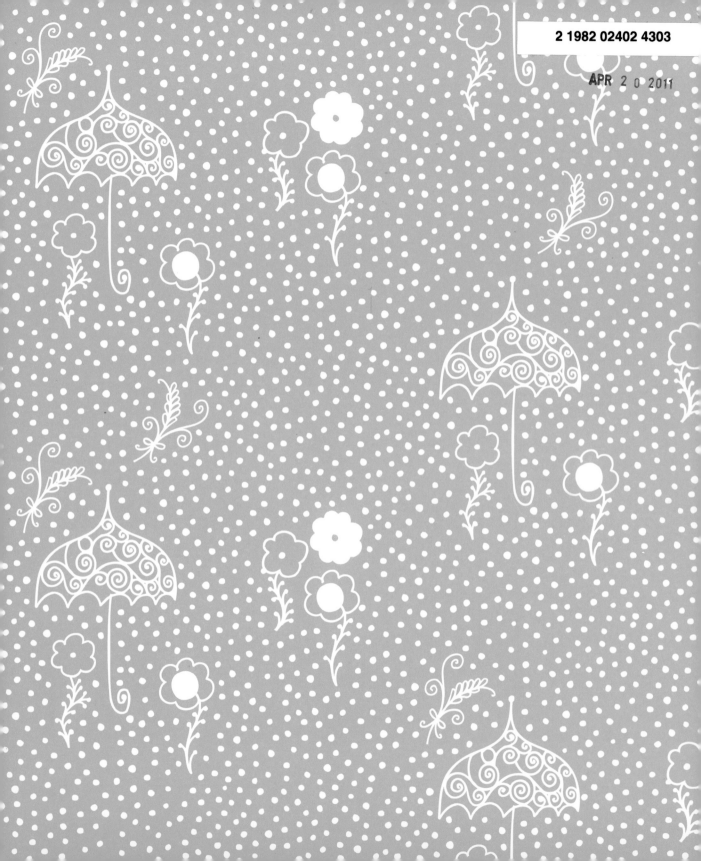